LUCY'S MASK

Lisa Sirkis Thompson

Illustrations by John Thompson

To all the workers in masks
who keep us healthy and safe.

First hardback edition June, 2021
ISBN: 978-0-5788-9702-8

For more information visit: **www.lucybookseries.com**

There's
nothing to do.

I can't even
see my friends.

There's nobody
in the whole
wide world to
play with.

I love masks!

With a mask...

...I can be whatever I want.
And nobody will know it's me.

I can be a detective!

I will solve a mystery.

I will search for hidden clues.

or...

I can be an explorer!

I will discover rare bugs.

I will hunt for lost cities

or...

I can be a pirate!

With a secret map.

I will find buried treasure.

or...

I can be a queen!

I will be kind to all my loyal subjects.

I will save them from fire breathing dragons.

or...

I can be a superhero!

I've been calling you.
I finished your mask.

This is a special kind of mask.
Let's try it on.

NOW you're a superhero!
With this kind of mask you really
will help save the world!

9 780578 897028